Great Gaudi

Written by Adam and Charlotte Guillain

It was the school holidays, and Asha and her friends took their sketchbooks to the museum.

"There are lots of interesting things to draw here!" said Asha's dad. "I've got a meeting now but I'll see you later."

"Look at these models!" Finn called.

"It says here a man called Antoni Gaudi made these," said Rav. "They're models of his buildings in Barcelona."

Asha began drawing one of the curving, colourful shapes.

"Hey, I can't see!" she cried as the lights flickered and dimmed.

We're going back in time!

The friends squeezed their eyes shut as they whirled away in the darkness. Then their feet hit the ground and they blinked in the bright sunlight.

"Where are we?" murmured Rav. A large city spread out below them and crickets chirruped all around.

"We're in a park," said Finn. "Hey, I recognise those buildings!" He pointed at two houses that looked like they were from a fairy tale.

"I think we're in Barcelona!" said Tess with a grin. "Let's explore."

The friends began racing around the park.

People were hard at work, building and decorating benches and walls.

"It's so beautiful!" said Asha as she traced the curving shapes with her hands. She gasped as a little lizard darted across the path.

The lizard scampered up on to the bench and closed his eyes as the sun warmed his skin.

"I'll catch up with you!" Asha called to her friends as she opened her sketchbook and began to draw the tiny creature.

Tess, Rav and Finn ran up some steps and disappeared into the trees. Meanwhile, Asha sat in the sunshine and sketched. Suddenly, a shadow fell over her as if a cloud had swept across the sky.

She turned and saw a man frowning at something. She followed his gaze. He was looking up at the steps of the park. She remembered the photo in the museum and excitement fluttered in her stomach.

"Excuse me," said Asha. "Are you Antoni Gaudi?"

The man turned and smiled. "Yes!" he said, shaking her hand.

The clattering noise of Asha's friends hurtling down the steps made them both look up.

"This is Mr Gaudi," Asha told them.

"Wow, pleased to meet you!" said Rav. The friends all introduced themselves.

"We love your park," said Tess. "Where do you get your ideas from?"

Gaudi smiled and said, "I love the colours and shapes in nature so I wanted to use them here. What do these blue tiles remind you of?"

Gaudi led them around the gardens to a wall where many people were working.

"It's a big mosaic," said Asha, watching them stick pieces of tile on to the wall.

"That's right," said Gaudi, smiling. "Would you like to help?"

"Yes please!" cried the friends.

They worked in the shade, following what the other people were doing. They were making good progress when Asha glanced up and saw Gaudi frowning at the steps again.

"What's the matter?" she asked.

"I want to put a fountain in the middle of the two flights of steps," replied Gaudi. "I just can't decide on the design for it."

Asha looked around the park. "What about a palm tree?" she suggested.

Gaudi shrugged. "Maybe," he sighed. "It might not be colourful enough, though."

He scratched his head and wandered off.

"Come on," Asha told her friends. "Let's find some ideas for Mr Gaudi's fountain."

That sounds fun!

They headed into the gardens. "He said the park is inspired by nature," said Rav. "I'm going to draw one of these flowers. Maybe he could design the fountain from that."

Tess sat on the path and started to draw some birds that were pecking in the dust.

"This plant's a good shape for a fountain," said Finn. He perched on a bench and started to sketch.

Asha sighed. "I really want to help," she thought. Then she yelped as a lizard like the one she'd drawn earlier ran across her foot.

As Asha jumped, she lost her grip on her sketchbook and it fell over the wall.

"Help!" she shouted, running out of the gardens. She watched in dismay as a gust of wind lifted up her sketchbook. The pages flew into the air!

Asha and her friends began to chase the pages through the park. Finn leaped up and grabbed a piece of paper before it fell into a puddle.

"Got one!" shouted Tess, snatching a page as it fluttered by.

Rav started to climb a tree to reach a page that was stuck in the branches, while Asha sped down the steps after another flying page.

"Help, Mr Gaudi!" she called when she saw him at the bottom. "My drawing!"

Gaudi flung out his hand …

… and caught the flapping sheet of paper.

"What's this?" he asked, flattening the sketch on a bench. Asha skidded to a standstill and watched him study her drawing. Her chest heaved as she struggled to catch her breath.

"It's perfect!" shouted Gaudi. He held up Asha's sketch of the lizard. "The fountain can come out of the lizard's mouth!"

Asha's stomach flipped with happiness, then she heard a shout.

"It's turning dark!" yelled Rav. "We're going back!"

Whizz! They were whirled back to the museum, where they stood facing Gaudi's models again.

"What's that really colourful model in the middle?" asked Tess, squinting through the glass.

Finn laughed. "It's a lizard," he said. "Asha's lizard!"

Talk about the story

Answer the questions:

1 Which city did the friends visit?

2 Why did Asha suddenly feel that excitement fluttered in her stomach? (page 9)

3 What does the word 'introduced' mean? (page 10)
Can you think of another word or some words that mean the same?

4 What did the friends help to make on the wall?

5 What did Rav draw, as an idea for the fountain?

6 How did Gaudi happen to see Asha's drawing? What did he decide when he saw the drawing?

7 Can you explain what the friends did to help Mr Gaudi?

8 Have you ever been to Spain? Did you like it? If you haven't been, would you like to go?

Can you retell the story in your own words?